D0431799

Sylvia Rose
and the
Cherry Tree

Sandy Shapiro Hurt
Illustrated by Xindi Yan

TILBURY HOUSE PUBLISHERS, THOMASTON, MAINE

Tilbury House Publishers
12 Starr Street
Thomaston, Maine 04861
800-582-1899 • www.tilburyhouse.com

Text © 2018 by Sandy Shapiro Hurt
Illustrations © 2018 by Xindi Yan

Hardcover ISBN 978-0-88448-527-8
eBook ISBN 978-0-88448-592-6

First hardcover printing January 2018

15 16 17 18 19 20 XXX 10 9 8 7 6 5 4 3 2 1

Library of Congress Control Number: 2017954443

Cover and interior designed by Frame25 Productions
Printed in China through Four Colour Print Group, Louisville, KY

For my sweet Dora Sabine, whose magic fills my branches, and for Eric, whose roots run deep next to mine. With thanks to my incredible, encouraging family, and to my muse, the real Sylvia Rose. —S.S.H.

To Laolao, my first art teacher and best friend. —X.Y.

This very strange tale began in May
in a friendly forest on a sunny day.

Skipping along a path in the wood
danced Sylvia Rose, and wow, she was GOOD!

Laughing and leaping came Sylvia Rose,
Whirling and twirling on twinkly toes.

She was instantly loved by the woodland creatures.
She had lovely manners and mischievous features.

But mostly the animals thought it a treat,
to see a young girl keep such a great beat.

As she danced to the tune of her very own song,
raccoons and chipmunks danced along.

Two doves, a fox, and two whippoorwills
spun and laughed—they couldn't sit still!

A granddaughter squirrel and a grandfather hare
danced as if they hadn't a care.

A mother owl and a honeybee
danced around the big cherry tree.

The animals never had had such fun.
They all joined in, one by one.

They begged and pleaded and made her agree
to meet the next day at the big cherry tree.

Then every day after she'd meet them to dance.
They'd wiggle and giggle and boogie and prance!

But a sigh of sorrow dampened their glee.
"What fun I am missing," moaned the big cherry tree.

"I bet YOU can dance!" cried Sylvia Rose.
"Your limbs wave like arms, and your roots curl like toes."

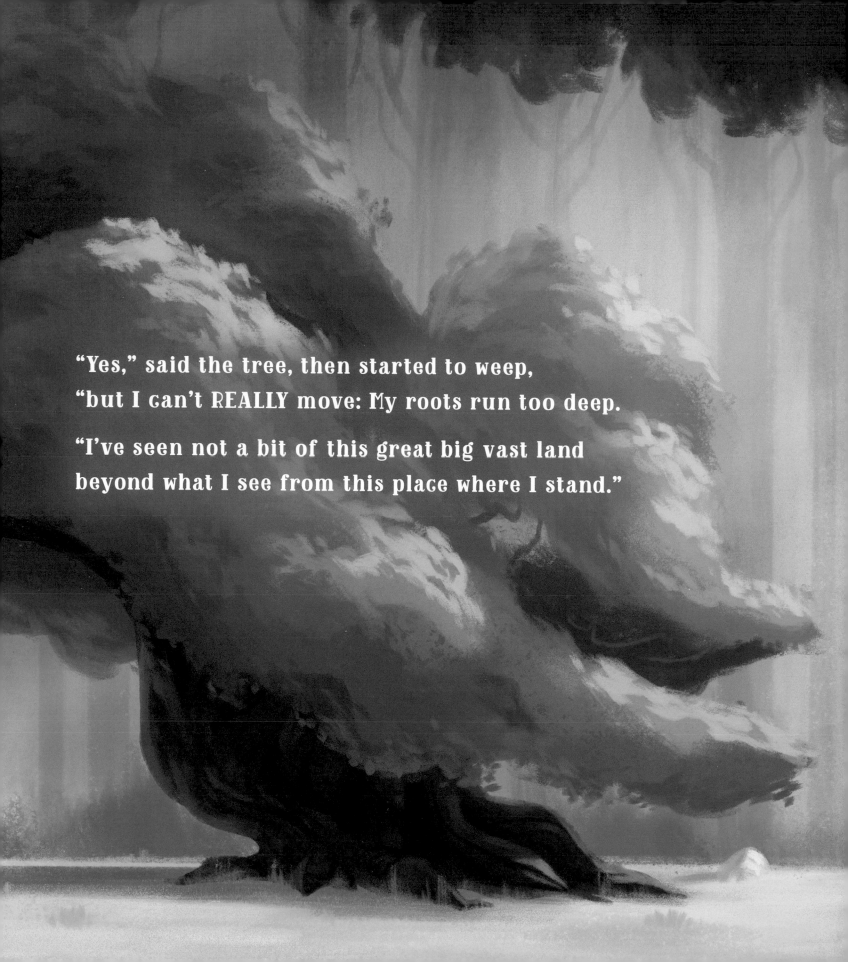

"Yes," said the tree, then started to weep,
"but I can't REALLY move: My roots run too deep.

"I've seen not a bit of this great big vast land
beyond what I see from this place where I stand."

The tree wept like a willow and pined like a pine,
sighed like a hemlock and drooped like a vine.

But Sylvia Rose remained optimistic.
They just had to figure out one great BIG logistic.

She climbed in the branches, the better to see
how one goes about moving a big cherry tree.

"I've got it!" she said. "Here's what must be done.
We'll dig up your roots from the ground one by one!

"We can all give a paw and it shouldn't take long.
We'll just dance as we do it and sing out a song!"

So they all went to work on the roots of the tree
and before very long it could dance and was free!

As it wiggled and giggled and shook all about,
Birds, bugs, and squirrels came tumbling out.

"I'll show you the world," said the girl to the tree.
"We'll dance all around it, there's so much to see!"

But the tree was concerned, and asked, "Do you think
we'll be able to stop for my roots to drink?"

"Why, of course." she replied, "No worries at all.
Without water, I know, you would dry up and fall!"

So they said their good-byes and joined branches in hands
to begin their adventures to faraway lands.

They danced to the desert for a very quick look,
then straight to the prairie to drink at a brook.

They danced to the seashore
and up a great mountain,

and to very old cities
where they drank
from old fountains.

They saw wonderful things as they spun and they twirled, the most wonderful things you can see in the world.

But back home the forest creatures had trouble.
They needed the tree to return on the double!

The sparrows who lived in the tree were dismayed.
Without their safe home they were tired and afraid.

The family of wood mites had run out of might,
with no wood to eat and a huge appetite.

The chipmunks were homeless, just like the rest.
For years the tree's trunk had hidden their nest.

The owl was exhausted. She was up day and night,
and could no longer get her whoo-whooing quite right.

Without their tree, they were all in great need,
but the creatures discussed it and finally agreed

that they'd give it more time, just a bit more to see
if they would all need to move to a new, different tree.

Indeed, they all said, it was better to wait.
It's SO hard to find good real estate!

So they banded together and labored like champs
to set up crude shelters and makeshift camps.

They hoped what they'd built would suffice for a bit,
and the tree would miss THEM the way they missed IT!

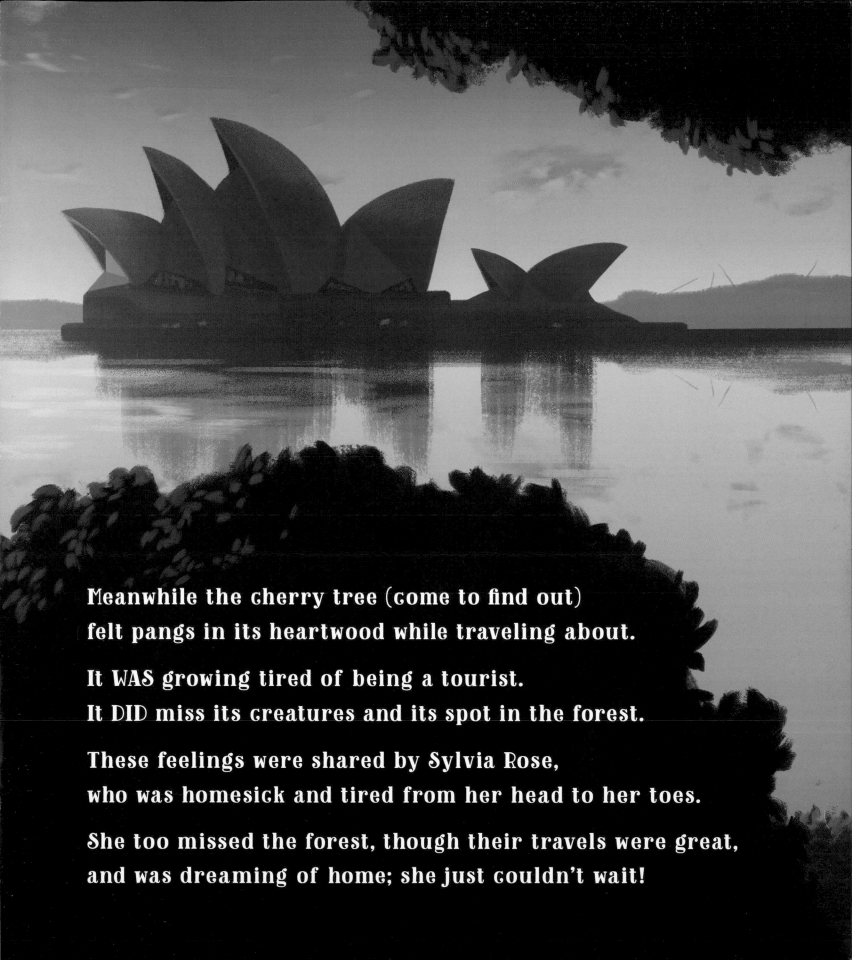

Meanwhile the cherry tree (come to find out)
felt pangs in its heartwood while traveling about.

It WAS growing tired of being a tourist.
It DID miss its creatures and its spot in the forest.

These feelings were shared by Sylvia Rose,
who was homesick and tired from her head to her toes.

She too missed the forest, though their travels were great,
and was dreaming of home; she just couldn't wait!

So they set off again with branches in hands
to make their way back to familiar lands.

They danced all day and all through the night,
till the edge of the forest they loved was in sight.

Imagine the joy! Imagine the glee,
when the creatures spotted the girl and the tree!

They sang and they danced like never before,
thrilled that the two had returned from their tour.

"It is swell" said the tree,
"to dance and to leap,
but oh, how I miss
my roots running deep!

"I shall never again take
my place here for granted.
Now, what do you say that we get me replanted?"

So that's what they did.
Every creature around
began digging and burying
roots in the ground.

They danced as they did it and sang out a song,
and the tree was rooted again before long.

Birds filled its branches, and chipmunks its trunk,
which they shared with a very nice new little skunk.

Wood mites got munching, cocoons were re-spun,
and it dawned on the tree how it loved everyone,

how the life in its limbs made it feel so complete,
and the spot where it stood was nothing but sweet!

But the story's not over, as you might suppose,
until we find out about Sylvia Rose.

When the forest was whole and complete once again,
and the creatures had homes, what did she do then?

Well they begged and pleaded and made her agree
to meet the next day at the big cherry tree.

And every day after, she met them and danced.
They wiggled and giggled and boogied and pranced.

On her twinkly toes on the path in the wood
danced Sylvia Rose, and wow, she was GOOD!

 Since her childhood in a Maine coastal forest, SANDY SHAPIRO HURT has been passionate about ecology and the abundant life the forest supports. She left Maine to pursue careers in the feature film industry and in event design and planning, but has returned to her roots with her husband, daughter, and a menagerie of chickens. This is her first children's book.

 XINDI YAN left behind her small city in China, traveling thousands of miles to New York City to realize her dream of being a published artist. She received her BFA in Illustration from Pratt Institute in 2013 and has since worked as an illustrator for the gaming industry and children's media while pursuing her passion as a children's book artist.